P9-BJG-642

SANDY SILVERTHORNE'S

SURVIVING ZITS

How to cope with your changing self

Standard
PUBLISHING
CINCINNATI, OHIO

Published in association with the literary agency of Alive Communications, Inc.,
7680 Goddard Street, Suite 200, Colorado Springs, Colorado, 80920.

ISBN 0-7847-1435-5

09 08 07 06 05 04 03   9 8 7 6 5 4 3 2 1

TABLE OF CONTENTS

YIKES!
WHAT'S HAPPENING AND WHY?

If you're asking yourself these questions, it can only mean one thing—you're growing up! Chances are, you're a little worried about preparing for dating, dealing with pimples, or some of that other stuff. That's OK because you won't grow up overnight. You'll get there by passing through a time-honored process called *adolescence*.

Sometimes kids who are at the beginning of the growing-up process worry about what's happening to them. The changes adolescents go through seem so strange! But, you can do and learn some things that will make the whole growing-up process easier. So this book has been designed to help you understand what's happening, give you some tips for getting through, and encourage you to become the cool person God has created you to be.

✳ adolescent: A person in the period of growing to adulthood. A teenager. Someone somewhere between puberty and adulthood.

✳ grown-up: A fully-grown person; an adult. Having reached the age of maturity (but they still might act immature on occasion). Characteristic of adults.

Your coming adolescence is a time when God's going to show you some cool things as you go from being a little kid to a grown-up. With God's help, you're going to be great!

Neal woke up to the reality
that alien life-forms were building a
civilization on his face . . .

BEWARE!

CHAPTER 1:

Body basics

PRIVATE

Keep Out!

WHAT'S A HORMONE?

So what exactly is causing all the puberty ruckus? The answer is hormones. A *hormone* is a chemical in your body that causes you to change. God created your body so that it would start making more and more hormones during puberty.

puberty: The period of life during which an individual becomes capable of sexual reproduction, and secondary sex characteristics (hair growth, body growth) start to develop.

These hormones are the chemicals that tell your body how to develop into an adult man or woman. They also signal other changes in your body. The first and most obvious change for most people is that they're growing. Big time.

NOW ENTERING
THE GROWTH ZONE

You've always been growing. You might even have been measuring yourself on the kitchen wall. And when you were six, seven, or eight, you probably grew 2 or 3 inches each year.

Well hold on, because you're about to enter a major growth zone that will take you up to your adult size! Some adolescents can grow up to 8 inches in one year! (Keep that up for the next four years, and we're talking a college sports scholarship of your choice!)

BUFFED OUT

Besides growing taller, guys, you'll notice your muscles are getting bigger and you'll start to get stronger. Those stronger muscles will help you be a lot better in sports— especially if you practice.

OOPS!

One side effect of growing quickly is that you may feel clumsy for a while. You might drop stuff or bump into the furniture or not be too great at sports. That's not very fun, but don't worry. This part of the process will pass as you grow into your body. You'll get used to being taller and having longer arms. With practice, you'll be more coordinated—a lot more. That's going to be fun.

OILY SKIN

Another change that will happen is your skin will feel a lot oilier. Your hormone production increases a little oil in your system called *sebum*.

Up to this point, the sebum was just hanging out, keeping your skin from getting too dry. Once you reach age 11 or 12, this stuff starts pumping oil to your face like the Alaskan pipeline. Then voila! You've got that dreaded teen disease more commonly known as . . . zits! Zits are a drag—especially if you've got a lot of them.

Kacey's Guide to
a Totally Awesome Complexion

Kacey's had to battle with her skin ever since she turned twelve. But she's figured out how to deal with oil, blemishes, and yeah, even zits. Here are five of her favorite skin tips.

1. Wash your face in the morning and evening using a mild soap and warm (but not hot) water. This gets rid of a lot of the grease and dirt that can cause acne. Dermatologists (skin doctors) also suggest using a product with benzoyl peroxide on your face after you wash.

2. Drink lots of water throughout the day. This is good for your skin and the rest of your body, too.

3. As tempting as it is to pop your zits, don't do it! This can cause scarring and it actually complicates your problem by pushing and spreading infection back inside your face. Gross!

4. Wash your hands—especially if you're going to be touching your face.

5. If it gets really bad, ask your parents if you can see a dermatologist. There are some really good medications that could make a big difference for you.

WHAT STINKS?

Along with all the other changes going on in your body, you're also going to be producing more oil and sweat. So if you don't watch it, you're going to, how can we say this . . . stink. Nobody's perfect, but if you want to keep your friends and make new ones, you'll have to deal with the "stink" factor.

Keep It Clean

Don't sweat it. Read these clean tips from Todd.

I used to think the other kids, and my teachers, and my parents, and, uh, even strangers were kidding when they all told me to take a shower. I took one every Saturday if I needed it or not! Then my dog stopped coming in my room. That convinced me that maybe I should clean up a little.

Getting rid of sweat is one of the easiest things to do. Just plan on taking a shower or bath at least every other day. Just turn on the water, get in, wash with soap (for real this time, not like you used to do when you just got wet), and rinse. It actually feels pretty refreshing. Then you're done.

Take it from me. When you're clean, you'll feel good. Your friends will feel good. And best of all, you'll smell good. You might also consider wearing deodorant or antiperspirant. Deodorant covers up the smell while antiperspirant actually stops the sweat. Talk to your parents or doctor about which one you might need.

I can do it all in about ten minutes. And guess what? I don't stink anymore. Cool!

BAD HAIR DAYS

You know what else puberty—and more specifically that sebum stuff—does? It makes your hair more greasy and oily. Oil in your hair can be good because it keeps it shiny. But during adolescence, you might find that your hair all of a sudden feels like you should be getting it styled at Minute Lube.

Oily hair is another problem that's easy to remedy. You'll probably just need to start washing your hair either every day or every other day. Use warm water and a little bit of shampoo. Work up a good lather, then rinse it off. Towel dry or use a hairdryer, but don't keep the heat on your hair too long or you might damage it.

Once your hair is nice and clean, try a couple of hairstyles to see which ones suit your face and personality. It's really up to you to find your own style. Just grab the hairdryer, choose some hair products, and shut the bathroom door.

Be creative. Try different things and find the "do" that's right for you!

SMILE! TAKING CARE OF YOUR TEETH

While we're at it, here's another friendly reminder: brush your teeth at least twice a day. Nobody wants to see what you had for breakfast every time you smile.

Use a medium-to-soft-bristle brush. Those are better for your gums. And change your toothbrush about every six months. That way you'll always have strong and effective bristles. It's also a good idea to visit your dentist twice a year for a check-up.

✴ Be true to your teeth...and they won't be false to you.

BRACE YOURSELF—DEALING WITH ORTHODONTIA

Adolescence is the time when a lot of kids get braces. You might be one of them. Hey, having braces on your face isn't the greatest thing in the world, but it's not the worst either.

Orthodontists can hide the braces or make them more fun. You might talk to your orthodontist (the braces doctor) about colored braces, white ones (that blend in with your teeth), or even invisible braces.

No matter which kind you get, make sure you follow your orthodontist's directions and you'll get them off sooner.

EXERCISE

Now that your body's doing all this growing, it's probably time to think about getting some exercise. Don't worry, we're not talking Navy SEAL training here. Actually, exercise can be fun. It helps you stay in shape and makes you feel better all day long.

Simple things such as walking to school, playing softball, riding your bike, or shooting hoops all count as exercise. Just get moving! You don't want to end up all sluggish like a couch potato.

FUEL FOR GROWTH—EATING RIGHT

What happens if you put maple syrup in your car's gas tank? Your car might run for a few blocks, but soon the car would totally break down. Just like your car, your body needs the right fuel to keep working and growing the way it's supposed to.

One more part of growing up is that you'll start to be responsible for deciding what to eat and what not to eat. Candy bars, pizza, French fries, burgers, and donuts sounds like a great menu. While all of those things are truly delicious and satisfying in their proper place, can you imagine what would happen if that's all you ate every single day?

Hey, we're not saying you can't enjoy some junk foods occasionally, but you probably don't want them to be your main diet.

You're smart and you want your body to be strong and healthy, so here's some information to help you make wise food choices. Check out the cool food pyramid to see if you're eating a good variety of foods.

What You Need to Know About Food Groups
by Todd

In my science class we studied this food pyramid. Let me see if I can remember how it works.

The bottom is stuff like breads and grains. Those kinds of foods have carbohydrates. Scientists think it's healthy to eat about six to 11 servings of these each day. Eating Toasty Oaties Cereal for breakfast is my favorite way to get a jump on this food group.

The next food group is fruits and vegetables. Of course, you want to eat a lot of these—at least five to seven servings a day. Brussels sprouts count as a vegetable, but I hate eating those, so I go with orange juice and carrots or apples and broccoli instead.

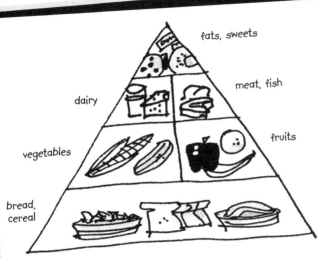

fats, sweets

meat, fish

dairy

fruits

vegetables

bread,
cereal

On the next level, you've got your meats, fish, eggs, nuts, and beans. These contain protein. My body needs protein to grow so I eat two or three servings of these each day.

Then there's the dairy group. Dairy means foods like milk and yogurt and stuff. These have calcium. That helps people get strong bones and teeth.

Then way up at the top (and you're not supposed to overdo it on these) are the sweets. Donuts and cookies and ice cream and candy bars and . . . well you get the idea.

So hey, if you eat like this pyramid says, you're going to get all the good stuff you need each day to grow big and strong. Like me.

CATCHING SOME ZZZZ'S

Growing up can really wear you out! Since you're growing so much and those hormones are flowing through your body, you may feel tired and sleepy throughout the day (our studies have found that math and history classes are particularly susceptible to daytime drowsiness).

To battle the exhaustion, you'll need to get plenty of sleep. You might be a "night owl" or maybe you like to get up with the chickens. Either way, make sure you get at least eight hours of sleep each night. Nine or ten hours is even better.

That means that if you get up at 7AM, you need to be in bed by 11PM if you want eight hours of sleep, 10PM if you want nine, and 9PM if you want ten hours of sleep. If you get on a regular sleep schedule, you'll feel great.

Flav's Suggestions for a Good Night's Sleep

Hi you guys. Before now, I wasn't ever too interested in going to bed. Too much to do, you know? But lately, I've been getting tired a lot (especially in French class right after lunch), so I've put together some tips on getting enough sleep.

1. Go to bed around the same time every night. That way your body will get on a schedule and you'll fall asleep faster.

2. Don't eat too much sugar or caffeine in the evening. Those things can keep you awake. (By the way, coffee and chocolate both have caffeine in them!) One time I ate four large chocolate bars right before I went to bed. Whoa, major insomnia!

3. Do something kind of quiet right before you go to bed, like reading or listening to music. It's really hard to go right to sleep after disco dancing or pole-vaulting.

SEXUAL CHANGES: GOD'S PLAN

In addition to growing taller and stronger and more adultlike, you go through some other physical changes that make you into a sexual being. These are the start of God's miraculous plan for moms and dads to be able to have children.

WHAT HAPPENS TO GUYS?
HAIR EVERYWHERE

One of the first things you'll notice is hair will begin to appear under your arms and in your groin area, too. Guys also might be growing hair on their faces. One of these days you'll need to start shaving.

When it is time to shave, don't sweat it. You can use an electric razor or shaving cream and a blade. The electric razor is pretty easy and might be the best way to start.

When you're done shaving, slap on a little aftershave lotion. It'll make you smell good, but it'll also help keep your skin smooth after each shave.

VOICE LESSONS

Another thing guys are going to notice—and for that matter, everybody else will notice, too—is that during puberty, your vocal cords will start to stretch and grow. (How else will you end up sounding like some cool actor like Sean Connery?)

As your vocal cords change, your voice will be changing, too. It's going to get deeper, but before that, it'll get squeaky. A guy starts to speak—or especially sing—and his voice makes a harsh, squawking sound, like a cat whose tail just got stepped on. It's like your throat doesn't know whether to go high or low, so it splits the difference and squeaks out like a parakeet caught in a tornado!

This is a real drag and can be incredibly embarrassing if it happens at the wrong time (like when you're giving a speech in your history class). Hang in there. It'll only last a few months.

DEALING WITH DESIRES

As guys reach puberty, their sexual desires start getting pretty strong. A lot of this is brought on by those hormones again (busy, aren't they?). You might find yourself thinking about girls 24/7. You might start having thoughts about a certain female (or a couple hundred) and wanting to kiss her and hold her and even experience sex with her.

Don't freak out! There's nothing wrong with you! These thoughts are a normal part of a guy's adolescence.

Growing up, getting interested in the opposite sex, marriage, kids, and the whole drill are all part of God's good plan for you. Yeah, the feelings are strong, but you still can be in control. It's not right to act on every feeling you have. Don't dwell on these new sexual feelings too much.

Start working now on learning to make good choices in the face of strong feelings. This is an awesome time to allow Jesus to capture your thoughts (see 2 Corinthians 10:5). The best way to combat overwhelming sexual feelings is to learn to think of girls as your friends, your sisters in the Lord, and as people worthy of the care and respect that God wants them to have.

WHAT HAPPENS TO GIRLS?

Any day now—sooner for some and later for others—girls your age are going to start looking and feeling more like women. One of the first changes you'll see is that hair will begin to grow under your arms and in your pubic area, too. You may want to start shaving your legs and your underarms.

Now don't be surprised if this kind of takes your mom by surprise (remember she might still feel like you're her baby). There might even be some . . . how can we say this . . . controversy about the subject. But be cool and open and get your mom's input. Show her the evidence! If your legs look all hairy—like you're wearing an army blanket—she may agree that it's time to do something about it. But if she thinks you should wait, you should respect that decision and follow her wishes (instead of secretly shaving them with friends at a slumber party on Friday night).

During puberty, girls will start to develop breasts. In fact, you'll probably notice that your whole body's starting to change shape—your hips might be getting a little wider, your body's filling out, and you're probably gaining some weight.

That's normal. In fact, it's great! But all these changes can make you feel like your body's out of whack. Some girls think there's something wrong with them or that they're getting fat.

Well hold on! Remember what we said about God creating you perfectly because he has plans for you? That includes your body, too. Of course it's good to eat right and take care of your body. But don't fall for the world's (and the devil's) lies that you have to look a certain way to be acceptable.

Magazines, TV, and hundreds of ads bombard your brain with the message that you must be 5' 9" and 105 pounds to be acceptable. No wonder girls start to worry when the shapes of their changing bodies don't match pictures of stick-thin models (which, by the way, have been airbrushed to the point of perfection).

God designed you to be exactly the way he wanted you to be, so don't start losing yourself in no-win comparison games.

GETTING YOUR PERIOD

Also during puberty a girl's body starts its menstrual cycle—she will have her first period. Getting your period is not dangerous and it doesn't mean anything is wrong. In fact, it's actually a sign that your body is healthy and growing right on schedule. Some girls will experience their first menstrual cycle as early as 11 years old, but most girls experience it between the ages of 12 and 14. This is all part of a miraculous plan that God has for girls to prepare for motherhood.

Even though this is just a simple explanation of what's going on, hopefully it'll give you some idea of the incredible way God's created your body. If you have questions or concerns, talk to your mom or dad, or an adult you can trust. Don't be afraid to ask questions.

WHAT IF NOTHING'S HAPPENING?

Sometimes it takes bodies a little while to get moving into puberty. Your friend may be 10 inches taller than you right now, and you're feeling like you'll never catch up. And while other people are discovering the opposite sex and stuff, you still feel—and look—like you're in the 4th grade! How frustrating!

So what's the hold-up? Everybody grows at the rate that's right for them. Our Creator planned it that way. Don't fret if you're taking more time to grow. Hang in there! Some kids don't get tall until high school, and some kids keep growing even in college!

TALK TO YOUR DOCTOR

If you're really concerned about your growth, talk to your parents or your doctor and they'll help you out. And if you're really skinny or starting to get overweight, the best remedy for that is eating better and getting some exercise. Talk to your PE teacher or coach about a workout you can do (or check out Coach Rorshauk's Fitness Challenge on page 88).

You   Your friend

REALITY CHECK

Adolescence has been part of God's plan for you since before you were born! Even though it's an awkward time in your life, it's also an awesome time. That's because you're taking steps towards being the grown-up person God wants you to be.

Have you ever thought about the fact that Jesus went through adolescence? His voice changed and he went through growth spurts, too. And if he went through all this, he understands what you're going through, too.

If you're feeling weird about the changes happening in your body, tell it to the Lord. Jesus knows about it, cares about it, and wants to help you through it. Take a moment and write down all the stuff you think is cool about growing up and all the stuff that you're worried about. Then tell the Lord about it.

BOTTOM LINE

You may not be the size you'd like to be right now, or as coordinated or as good-looking, but hang in there! God's plans for you are perfect. In fact, write down this verse and hang it on your mirror. Every time you look at yourself, read this promise from God. That way, you'll start to see yourself the way God sees you.

I will praise You,
for I am fearfully and wonderfully made.
Psalm 139:14

For some reason, Matt is having
difficulty focusing in class...

BEWARE!

CHAPTER 2:

The emotional roller coaster

PRIVATE

Keep Out!

Whatever things are true, whatever things are noble,
whatever things are just, whatever things are pure,
whatever things are lovely . . . meditate on these things.
Philippians 4:8

RIDING THE EMOTIONAL ROLLER COASTER

God designed humans to be very complex. The physical, emotional, and even spiritual parts of our bodies affect one another. Puberty really gets all three of those parts going. You remember those hormones we talked about? Well those same hormones that are helping make your body grow can affect your moods as well.

Do you ever find yourself going through the day feeling really happy—almost silly—one moment, then kind of depressed or worried for a while, and then really mad over something later? Well a lot of what you're feeling right now is a result of the physical changes going on in your body.

Actually, that is the good news. A lot of the strong emotions that you feel in adolescence are made stronger by the hormones in your body. So even if it feels like the world's about to come crashing down around you, trust us, it isn't. Once you get past adolescence, most of the intense feelings that you may be experiencing will be much less intense. If you find yourself going through some emotional ups and downs, hang in there. These are normal.

THE TRUTH OF THE MATTER

When you're feeling overwhelmed by a confusing or especially strong emotion (like anger or sadness) try these three things:

1. Watch your mouth. Yeah, this is hard but you'll be glad you didn't say something you'll regret later. Often we say some pretty rude or mean things when we're feeling bad, so watch what you say.

2. Slow down and try to think about what's really bothering you. Take a walk or get alone for a few minutes. Then think about this: are you overreacting to a small thing? Chances are your hormones are making you feel worse.

3. Talk to God about it. He really wants to know what's going on with you, as well as help you through it. He is someone you can trust. Just pour out your feelings to God.

You want to know a secret? OK, here goes. Most people you know feel a little insecure about themselves sometimes. Yup, even your friends, teachers, and coaches feel that way. The guy at the mini-mart, big-time executives, supermodels, and even football stars feel like other people have got it all together and they don't.

This feeling is especially strong during adolescence because you're at the age where you're trying to figure out who you are and what makes you tick! Figuring that out is cool, but tricky.

The devil likes to take advantage of your sometimes mixed-up feelings and starts feeding you lies about yourself and the world around you. And you sure don't want to get sucked into that game!

Truth Vs. Lies: A Simple Guide

Here's a short list of some of the lies you might run into. Have you heard any of these before? Don't be fooled! God's Word will tell you the real story here.

Lie: God doesn't even know who you are. And he doesn't care about you.

Truth: OK this lie really makes God mad because it's a lie about you and him. Check out Isaiah 49:15. "Can a woman forget her nursing child, and not have compassion on the son of her womb? Surely they may forget, yet I will not forget you."

Now think about that. This Bible verse asks the question, "Could a mom forget her little kid?" The answer is of course not! You're God's child. He will not forget you, either! God cares about every little thing in your life. He wants the very best for you every day.

Do you need more proof? God sent his only son to die for you so that you and God could be best friends forever. So when you start to feel like God doesn't know or care about you, check out his Word and tell him how you're feeling.

Lie: You're ugly and your body's a loser.

Truth: Feeling unattractive can be painful. It can even suck the life out of you. If this lie is getting to you, you're not alone. A lot of people feel this one.

Here's the thing. God doesn't make mistakes. He created you. He loves you just as you are. Those facts alone make you (and your body) beautiful.

God's a lot more interested in what's going on in your heart than what's going on in the mirror. Don't get too caught up in your physical appearance.

Lie: Nobody likes you.

Truth: Although this may be a lonely time for you (and for a lot of people!) the truth is there are a lot of folks who like you. I mean, what's not to like? You're smart, good-looking, and very cool. And you belong to the Creator of the whole universe! If he thinks you're awesome, it's just a matter of time before others notice it, too.

Try being a good friend to someone. When you start treating others like you'd like to be treated, good friendships will start to develop.

Lie: Life stinks and it's always going to be this way.

Truth: This is the biggest lie of them all. The enemy of our souls (the devil) wants you to get so overwhelmed by your situation that you forget that God is bigger than anything you ever face. Whenever things get confusing or difficult, ask God for help. He can take things that seem hopeless, breathe his life into them, and turn things around.

Trust him, do what he tells you to do, and hang in there. Remember God's a whole lot bigger, stronger, and greater than anything in the world (1 John 4:4).

WHAT DO I DO?

So what do you do to handle these intense feelings? What should you do when you're mixed up? Just follow this expert advice. Raise your right hand and repeat after us:

"I _____ (state your name), promise that when something's bugging me, I will talk to someone about it. I realize that if I hold it all in, I might explode."

MY TEAM

You've just promised to talk to someone about your feelings. But who will you call? You need someone who's "been there" and can help. The only other requirements are that this person should love God and love you.

Start thinking about some cool people you know who could help. Look at it as making a team who will be there to show you how cool life can be and to help you through the tough times. Your team could be made up of your youth pastor, a Sunday school teacher, one of your favorite camp counselors, or an older Christian kid.

Godly input, love, and support are wonderful gifts from God. When you're up against some of the challenges life might throw at you, members of your team can just listen and say, "We understand."

Adolescence is a hard time for most people. Lots of kids—even kids with good friends and parents on their teams—struggle with feeling lonely or angry or depressed.

If you're experiencing several of these symptoms you might be depressed:

Not interested in friends or activities
Blowing off your schoolwork
Feeling sad and hopeless a lot
Major anger or rage
Feeling really bad about yourself
Low energy
Changes in your eating or sleeping patterns
Abusing alcohol or drugs

If you feel depressed a lot of the time or for a period longer than a couple of weeks, you need to talk to someone about it. Your mom or dad or school counselor or youth pastor would be glad to help.

Honor your father and your mother. Exodus 20:12

FEELINGS ABOUT YOUR PARENTS

Ever since you were born, you've pretty much relied on your parents for everything. Your parents chose what you would eat, where you would go, and what you would wear. One day, when you're an adult, all of those choices will be yours. Right now, you're somewhere in the middle.

You are here

Every year as you get older, you're going to gain a little more independence and responsibility. You get the chance to be in charge of more and more decisions that affect your life.

But your parents are still in charge overall. The problem comes when you and your parents don't agree on some decision. You want to go one way and they don't! That's frustrating! The hormones racing through your body are making your feelings about the situation even stronger and making the frustration even worse. Believe it or not, this problem happens to parents and kids everywhere.

INDEPENDENCE

One of the first places where parents and adolescents disagree is the area of self-expression. Instead of being Mom and Dad's little girl or boy, you're going to want to be, you know, just you! You're going to want to let the world know who you are, what you're like, and what you're good at.

That's great. You are a special, unique creation of God. He wants you to be who he created you to be. What you have to watch out for is how you choose to express yourself. How do you want to present the new, changing YOU to the world . . . and what if your parents don't agree with your choice?

EXPRESS YOURSELF

Lots of kids get to this stage and are just dying to make a wild statement by dyeing their hair blue or red. Or maybe you're thinking of piercing your ears, eyebrows, and lips!

Are you ready to shock the world with a bold new look? If you're wanting to change your look in this radical way, first ask yourself, "Why am I doing this?" Is it to fit in? Are you thinking of getting that tattoo just so people will notice you? Be honest with yourself about it and then decide if the reason is good enough.

God doesn't really talk too much about hair color or body piercing in the Bible, but he is pretty clear about honoring your parents. If your parents hate this idea (and let's face it, they will HATE this idea), then you need to drop it.

Looks Can Be Deceiving
by Kacey

Hey, it may not be your style to get pierced or tattooed, but chances are some of the kids around your school might choose to do it. Does that make them bad? No way! They've just got different taste than you, and that's how they're expressing who they are.

Try going through a week (or even a day) without judging what a person is like by the way he or she looks. In other words, start looking at other kids the way God does. First Samuel 16:7 says that God doesn't look at a person's appearance; he looks at the heart. Who knows? You may find some really cool, fun people underneath all the purple hair and nose rings.

YOU'RE WEARING THAT!

Girls, you've picked out a really cool outfit, but your mom thinks it shows too much skin. Guys, you're into the grunge look, but your dad thinks you look like a slob. "No child of mine is going to be seen like that in public!" Welcome to the "Wardrobe Wars."

It's hard when your friends have the latest clothes and you're feeling major pressure to fit in. Don't worry! Your folks may have some good ideas on where to shop for affordable, tasteful clothing that will allow you to be yourself. What you're wearing may feel like the most important thing right now, but keeping respect and love in the house is a lot more crucial.

BORN TO ROCK! MUSIC WARS

Another area of disagreement between kids and their parents that dates back to the beginning of time is music.

Your parents may have some guidelines about what music you can listen to and how loud it can be. And your parents' guidelines may be more strict than the ones your friends' parents have given them.

Your folks are probably not going to enjoy a lot of your music, but remember they're the ones who are supposed to take care of you. If they say no to some of your music choices, they're just doing their job.

Remember—you get to honor them even if you don't always agree with them.

✳ Listening to songs about drugs, weird sexual stuff, and killing people is a little like drinking small amounts of poison and hoping it won't hurt you. Hey, there's a lot of cool, hip music out there that doesn't get into all that stuff. Check it out.

GETTING ALONG

Those are just some of the things you might disagree
with your parents about. So how do you deal with
this "my-parents-don't-want-to-let-go-but-I-need-
some-independence" thing? (That's the scientific
term for it.) Can you honor your parents and still
grow into yourself?

The answer is yes. Just ask Eddie how he does it.
He has some ideas you might try to make things
a little more peaceful at home.

Eddie's Tips for Peace on Earth
(at least at your house)

You'll probably find this hard to believe, but a couple
of years ago my mom and I had a few, um, minor
disagreements. In my opinion she totally overreacted
to the smallest things. I mean a lot of 13-year-olds
have their own condo on the beach in Mexico!

Anyway, my mom and I have figured out a few ways
to start talking and get back on the same team.

1. Try sitting down with your parents (with no brothers and sisters or friends around) and telling them what's going on with you. You might even write down some of the things you want to say. Talk to them calmly and respectfully and let them know how you're feeling. Listen to what they have to say, too.

Make your requests, but be realistic. You may want to stay out until 11 and they may want you home at 9, so maybe compromise with 9:30 or 10. Be prepared to ask for what you want, but accept what they want for you.

You've probably discovered by now that yelling doesn't usually get what you want. After all, they are the parents—they own the house and the car—so they do have the final say on stuff.

2. As your parents begin to give you more and more freedom, show them that you can be responsible with it. If they let you go to a football game and tell you to be home by 10, do it! As they see that they can trust you, they'll feel more and more comfortable giving you more and more freedom.

3. Pray together with your parents. One of the coolest things you can do together is go to the One who created the whole universe and let him know what's going on. The Bible says he's the same "yesterday, today, and forever" (Hebrews 13:8), so he wants to help you through whatever you and your folks are going through right now. Try it. He'll work wonders.

RESPONSIBILITY

Now that you're growing older, smarter, and totally cool, your parents are probably going to give you some new responsibilities. Maybe you're staying home alone after school, or doing more chores around the house. Maybe you're responsible for bigger stuff like mowing the lawn or even making some meals.

Having more responsibilities is really cool because it's like practicing for when you're grown-up and on your own. You'll start learning stuff like finishing what you start, and taking pride in your work. These are skills that will help you succeed when you're older.

Having your own money may be another new responsibility for you. And this is a good time to talk to your parents about money.

✷ Here's a good money tip: Save 10 percent for later, give 10 percent to God (you know, you church or a Christian organization) and use the rest.

Do they give you an allowance every week? Do they pay you for individual jobs? Getting a little cash for doing a good job can be good motivation for working and it'll give you a chance to learn about saving and spending.

FIGHTING AND MAKING UP

You may have already had conflict, arguing, hurt feelings, and general misery. Like it or not, this is part of the process. OK, so you didn't read Eddie's tips in time and you and your parents just had a huge fight. What should you do?

First, realize that everybody's going through this. In fact all up and down your street, throughout your city, across the U.S.A., and even in foreign countries, parents and kids are going through disagreements.

The second thing is, although your parents might be pretty upset with you right now, they don't hate you or wish you didn't live with them or anything like that. It might feel that way, but it's just not true.

Being in both the "kid" world and the "grown-up" world is hard for you, but it's hard on your parents, too! Your parents want you to grow up, but they still want to protect you, too. And, even if this has become really miserable, with yelling and hurt feelings and stuff, your parents still love you and want the best for you.

Your parents are realizing that you're growing up and you're not their little baby anymore, and that may be hard for them.

It's hard for parents to let go because they know there is a lot of bad stuff out there in the real world and they want to protect you from all of it.

When you were little, they could just put you in the car, give you an ice cream cone, and take you home where you'd be safe and happy. But now they're seeing that you're making more and more of your own decisions and that scares the pants off of them! They worry that you're going to make mistakes and wrong choices. And because they love you, they don't want you to have to go through all that.

You and your parents are trying to figure out how this whole independence thing is going to look. And you know who can help you all work it out for the best? God can! You may have to play your part and be the first one to apologize, but this may be the first step in God getting things back on track. It really doesn't matter who started it, so is this argument worth losing your relationship with your folks? Probably not. So you may have to make the first move in reconciliation. Go ahead. Ask God to help you. He will, you know.

 REALITY CHECK

This whole "honor your parents" thing may be one of the biggest challenges you'll face as you grow into adolescence. This might be because it seems really uncool to do it, or because your friends don't seem to honor their parents.

The world around us doesn't really encourage us to honor our parents either. But God sure takes it seriously enough. After all, he's got it as number five in his original Top Ten (Commandments, that is. Check it out in Exodus 20:12!).

Luke 2:51 says that even Jesus was "subject [obedient] to" his parents. Think about that. The One who created the heavens and the earth (and yes, even his parents!) knew it was right to obey them. That's how God set it up. It won't always be easy, but God wants to help you do it. Just ask him. Next time you and your parents aren't getting along too well, pray to your heavenly Father. Ask him to help you guys love, respect, and honor one another. If you do your part, he'll do his.

BOTTOM LINE

Respecting your parents and honoring them is an act of faith and trust in God. It means you're saying to God, "I don't understand this or even agree with it right now, but I trust you to take care of me—and this situation—as I follow you and do what you want me to do."

Love one another fervently with a pure heart.
1 Peter 1:22

FEELINGS ABOUT THE OPPOSITE SEX

Just when you thought that your hormones had inflicted all the damage they could possibly do, there is something else. Now that your body is getting ready to grow into a mother or father, your emotions and feelings are moving in that direction, too. As you get older, you're going to become interested in the opposite sex. That's also part of God's plan.

The Hormone-O-Rama

JUST 4 GUYS

Sexual desires—that attraction you feel for the opposite sex—are good. In fact, God gave you those desires. But like any good gift, we can really mess things up by misusing it. If you follow God's plan for this area of your life and wait until you're married to enjoy sex, your life will be much richer. Guaranteed.

No one your age is really ready to have a girlfriend. Don't let your feelings carry you into a heavy relationship that's not good for you or her. Instead of dating, do stuff in a group. Make friends with girls and enjoy them for who they are—not for what you want out of them.

Because they're thinking about girls a lot, some guys may start to worry that there's something wrong or even sinful about their desires. Some guys get the wrong idea and think that God's pretty disgusted with them. They worry that God thinks they're freaks.

First, as we've said, sexual desires are perfectly normal. God created us to be attracted to the opposite sex and that's his cool plan for each of us. So if you're thinking about girls all the time, don't worry, you're *not* a freak.

But the Bible does say to take our thoughts captive to the Lord (remember 2 Corinthians 10:5?). That basically means to give God control over our thought-life and realize that we can choose what to think about. If you're having trouble getting your thoughts under control, tell God about it and ask him to help you.

JUST 4 GIRLS

You may have avoided guys like the plague for most of your life, but you'll come to a point when suddenly they're starting to look, well, not so bad. This is a natural part of growing up and entering adolescence, and God created you to be this way.

It's a wonderful feeling when you have your first crush. It's exciting to like a guy. And if that boy likes you back, that's even better.

But while you're probably going to be much more interested in who the boy is, guys are going to get into how you look and walk and stuff. Guys and girls are different that way.

Guys struggle with strong sexual desires in a way that's different from the feelings girls have. Take care not to cause your guy friends or your "crush" to think inappropriate sexual thoughts about you.

For the most part, relationships and the boyfriend/girlfriend thing will be much more meaningful to you than it is to a guy. Girls tend to value relationships more and work hard to get to know a person inside and out. Guys your age aren't ready to have a girlfriend, so the best thing you can do is to remain friends.

TO DATE OR NOT TO DATE

In spite of what TV or magazines, or even your friends may say, don't feel like you need to start dating right away. Relationships between guys and girls are much better when you're older.

It's not always easy to wait for things to happen. If you're worried about dating, or if you wish you had a boyfriend or girlfriend, take a look at what Psalm 37 has to say.

Trust in the Lord, and do good . . . Delight yourself also in the Lord, and he shall give you the desires of your heart. Commit your way to the Lord, trust also in him . . . Rest in the Lord, and wait patiently for him.
Psalm 37:3-7

The best thing you can do right now is to enjoy members of the opposite sex as your friends—and your brothers and sisters in the Lord. Later, when the time comes, you can develop deeper friendships and even head toward dating and marriage.

 REALITY CHECK

God gave the gift of sex to men and women as a way of enjoying this life he's given us, and of course, for continuing the human race. But God also designed sex to be between people who are married to each other and nowhere else. Sexual activity in any other context never works out. It hurts us emotionally, spiritually, and sometimes even physically.

So no matter how strong your feelings may be, the only way we'll really experience the full life God has designed for us is to obey him and trust him in every area of our lives. And that includes the sexual part.

Decide right now how you'll handle sexual temptation. Talk about it to your parents or your pastor or youth leader. If you decide right now that you're going to hold off on your sexual activity until marriage, it'll be much easier for you to avoid tempting situations.

BOTTOM LINE

You're you, so don't try to be anyone else no matter what the world says. Always remember that God knows what you're going through (in fact he created it). He's also got great plans for you—and your relationships. So no matter where you are in this relationship thing just focus on getting to know God better. Let him into every area of your life, then all this other stuff will fall into place.

But seek first the kingdom of God and His righteousness, and all these things shall be added to you.
Matthew 6:33

Joel is getting good at
sending voice mail . . .

BEWARE!

CHAPTER 3:

Spirit matters

PRIVATE

Keep Out!

The Spirit gives life. 2 Corinthians 3:6

GOT SPIRIT?

We've talked about what's happening with your body, your emotions, how much you're growing, and even your zits, but what about the most important part of your whole being? What's happening with your spirit?

If you've told Jesus that you want him to be the leader (or Lord) in your life, then you're off to a good start. But now that you're growing and changing, you have a new challenge—how to make your relationship with Jesus grow with you.

When you were younger, your relationship with the Lord was kind of "done for you" by your parents. You know, they may have taken you to church, helped you pray, and taught you about the Bible and stuff. But as you move into adolescence, you get to take charge of this relationship.

God wants to become more and more involved with you personally. And he wants you to know him better, too. Do you know ways to get more of God in your life? Read Todd's article on the next page for some tips.

Can't-Miss Suggestions for Getting to Know God
by Todd

Hey, what's up? You know I've been a Christian since I was about four years old, but this year something new is happening. It's weird, but it's like Jesus is showing me who he is in new ways.

It's not spooky and I'm not hearing voices or anything. When I'm at church, or when I read the Bible, it's like he's really talking to me. It's so cool!

Anyway here's some stuff you can do to grow in your relationship with the Lord.

Instant message with him

Get a Bible. Get a version you can read and understand. Ask your mom, dad, or youth leader to help you get one. Then read some every day—even if it's just a chapter or so. Let God teach you about himself and how he wants you to live.

I recommend the gospel of John in the New Testament as a starting point. That book talks about Jesus when he was on Earth about 2000 years ago.

Instant messaging part 2

Spend some time in prayer every day. Don't worry about how you sound or about using all the right words. Just talk to him like you would a really cool, loving friend. Tell him everything—the stuff you've done wrong, the things you're thankful for, the things you're worried about . . . everything.

Family time

If you want to grow spiritually, make it a point to hang out with other kids who love God. Make friends at church or in a small group.

Me, Flav, and Eddie get together once a week with one of our youth leaders for a Bible study and sharing time. It's cool to just be myself and talk to these guys about the Lord and stuff. You should do that, too.

LIKE JESUS

Todd's tips are all good ways to become closer to God. Another way is through serving others—just like Jesus did.

The Bible says that Jesus came to serve, not to be served (see Matthew 20:28). So if we're going to be like him, we should, you know, serve. You don't have to wait until you're a grown-up to serve others. You could try something like mowing a neighbor's lawn or helping some kid with his homework or sports practice or something. Just ask God to show you opportunities to help, and keep your eyes open. God will show you how to do it.

Another way to serve people is to tell them about what God has done in your life. Just be honest. Let them know what a cool God you serve.

SO, HOW DOES GOD WANT ME TO SERVE HIM?

Here's the cool part! God wants you to discover your gifts, develop them, and learn how to use them for him. You might be saying, "What can I possibly do for God?" Well, slow down. Look around. What do you like to do?

One way to figure out the gifts God's given to you is by discovering the stuff you enjoy the most. Do you like to cook? Draw? Play football? Work with animals, or little kids? Then chances are God's gifted you in that area and he can use those talents to help and encourage other people. Here's what to do:

1. Ask God to show you the special gifts and talents he's given you.

2. Make a list of the things you love to do.

3. Figure out how God might have you use your gifts. (For example, if you like to work with kids, you could be a coach or teach Sunday school.)

4. Practice your skill! Be the best you can be at your gifts!

Whoa! There's so much to think about as you enter this stage of your life! Just remember that adolescence is a cool time to open up your spirit to God even more than before.

The number one thing on God's wish list is to get to know you better. He's not going to force you, so he'll wait until you invite him in. In Revelation 3:20 Jesus says, "I stand at the door and knock." He's waiting for us to open up our hearts, and allow him to come in and be involved in every part of our lives.

You
Are
Here

BOTTOM LINE

God wants to use his people to help you figure this stuff out. So grab some cool Christian friends and hang on . . . it's going to be a fun ride!

This is your worst nightmare...

BEWARE!

APPENDIX:

Coach Rorshauk's fitness challenge

PRIVATE

Keep Out!

Your body is the temple of the Holy Spirit . . . therefore, glorify God in your body. 1 Corinthians 6:19, 20

APPENDIX

"Exercise is good for you!" "Why don't you stop watching television and go outside and play?" "Drop and give me 50!" (Just kidding—that is unless you have Coach Rorshauk as your PE teacher.)

No way! I don't want to run or do stuff like that! Exercise is too painful!

Sounds painful, doesn't it? Well, this section deals with keeping strong and healthy through—you've got it—exercise and activity.

EXERCISE

Nobody started playing the guitar like a rock star the first time they picked it up, or shot 30 three-pointers the very first time they stepped onto a basketball court. It took time—and practice—to get good at both of those things. Well, guess what? Exercise is just like everything else in life. You have to start right where you are and build from there.

Drop and give me 50!

So if you can't do 50 push-ups or 100 sit-ups or any pull-ups, don't worry! Just hang in there. Start off small, stick with it, and pretty soon you'll find yourself able to do all these things. Plus your body will feel better, too.

Don't know where to start? We asked nationally recognized youth fitness authority and former Marine drill instructor Arnie (Coach) Rorshauk to put together a little workout plan you can follow at home.

Coach Rorshauk's Fitness Challenge for Guys and Girls

All right you kiddies, I'm going to whip you into shape. I'm going to take you through some grueling exercises that I learned during my stint in the Marines. Boy those were the days. I remember being stationed down in . . . never mind.

Where was I? Oh, yeah, if you keep this routine up three or four times a week, you're going to be fit as a fiddle. By the way, before you do any of these exercises you'll need to get in some comfortable clothes, like shorts and a tee shirt.

1. The Push-Up

Now you've probably all seen these babies once or twice. These are a great way to strengthen your arms and upper body. Check this out:

Lie face down on the floor with your hands straight out from your shoulders about 6 inches. (Figure one)

Now push that puny little body of yours up until your arms are straight. (Figure two)

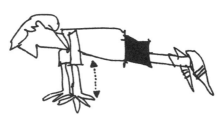

Try to keep your back straight as you do this. Now lower your body until you're about 5 inches from the floor. Then up again. Now I want you to do 500 of these puppies. Go! Just kidding! Start out with five or six. Try to build up to 10, then 15 or 20.

OK, OK, I hear ya' whining. You're saying, "I can't do that! These are hard!" Hey, I never said these were going to be a walk in the park. But there is a little secret. If you can't do them the way I just explained, start out by keeping your knees down on the floor. (Figure three)

You might be saying, "But that's cheating!" Hey, do you want to learn how to do these or not? Listen, if you strengthen your arms and shoulders by doing these little lightweight push-ups for a while, pretty soon you'll be doing the real thing. Trust me. It's all about getting in shape.

2. Crunches

These little hummers are a great way to strengthen your abs (or stomach muscles). Here's what you do:

Lie on your back on the floor with your knees bent. (Figure four)

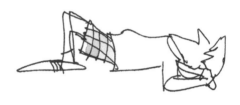

Put your hands behind your head for support. Now slowly raise your shoulders off the floor towards your knees, using your stomach muscles to pull you up. (Figure five)

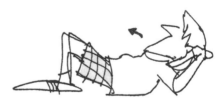

Don't come up too far—only about 4 inches off the floor. Then slowly lower yourself back down. Do about five of these to start. Try to work up to 15 or 20.

3. Jumping Rope

Yeah, I know, you're saying, "This is for little girls!" Well obviously you've never seen a heavyweight boxer training for a fight. You try jumping rope for 5 minutes straight. It's hard! Anyway, who's the coach around here, you or me?

Just grab a jump rope and start jumpin'. (Figure six)

It's one of the best aerobic exercises you can do. And besides that, it's good for your heart, too. Like the other exercises we're doing, start out slow. Just go for a couple of minutes at first and work up.

Do these three exercises— and do 'em right—three to five times a week. Well, this is Coach Arnie Rorshauk saying keep your head up and your mouth shut or you're going to be running some laps. See ya soon!

 REALITY CHECK

You know what? God has set it up so that if we are faithful and take care of the gifts he's given us, then he'll bless us and give us more to take care of. One of the most important gifts God has given to you is your body. If you take good care of it by eating right most of the time, exercising, getting enough sleep, and bathing occasionally, not only will you grow up right, but you'll also learn something about God's plans for you.

Taking good care of your body requires some discipline (just ask Coach Rorshauk!) and self-control. But you don't have to rely totally on your own strength to get the job done. God promises to help you be self-controlled if you rely on his Spirit inside of you.

Are you taking good care of yourself? Take a minute and write down some of your thoughts on this subject.

Good things I'm already doing:

_____

_____

_____

What I'd like to start doing:

_____

_____

_____

Stuff I think God would like me to quit: (Lord, I need your help to do this!)

_____

_____

_____

BOTTOM LINE

When we do our part, God will do his part. Then amazing things will happen!

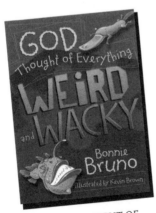